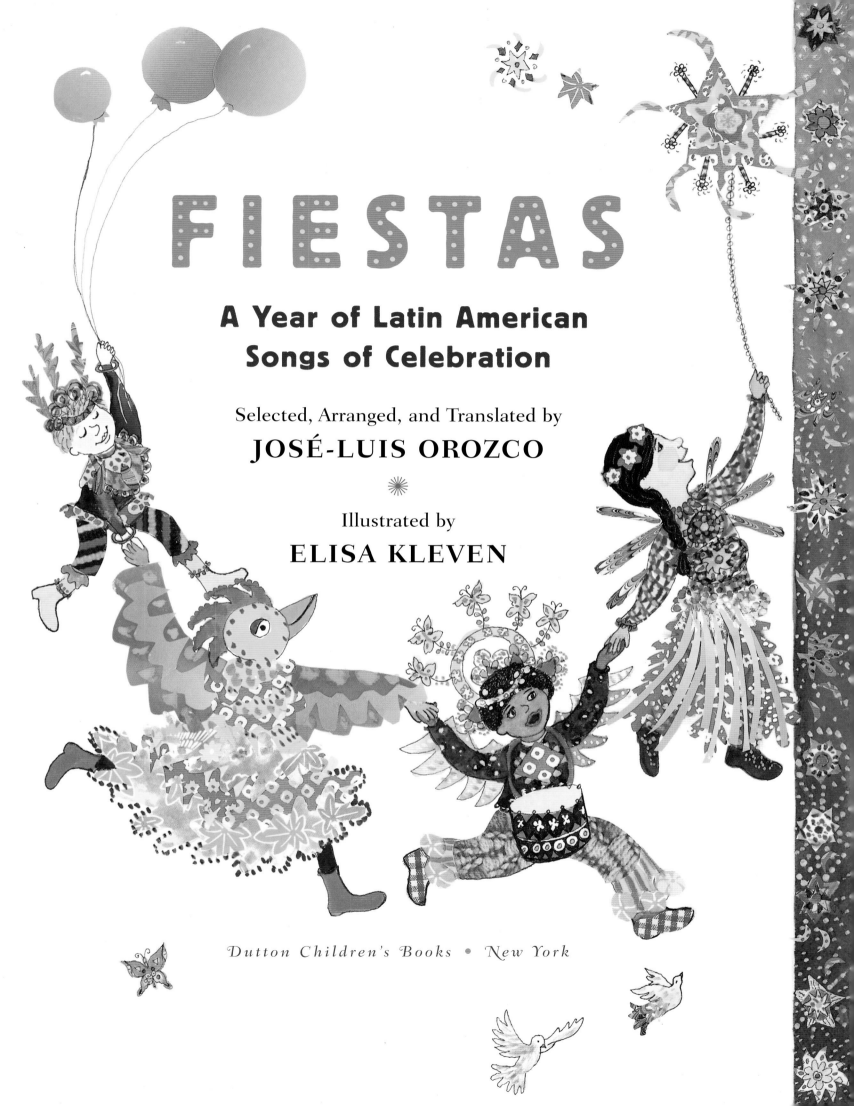

FIESTAS

A Year of Latin American Songs of Celebration

Selected, Arranged, and Translated by

JOSÉ-LUIS OROZCO

*

Illustrated by

ELISA KLEVEN

Dutton Children's Books • New York

Para mi nieto Ometeotl
In memory of Doctor Marcos Guerrero and José Antonio Burciaga, dos grandes amigos
To all teachers, librarians, parents, and children
Special thanks to Kendra Marcus, Roberto Chiofalo, and Joyce Williams
—J.-L.O.

To my festive siblings, Carol, Bill, Susie, Larry, Gail, Tom, Cathy, Noel,
Merry, Sylvia, Herb and Sue
Special thanks to Alissa Heyman and José-Luis Orozco
—E.K.

CIP Data is available.

Published in the United States 2002 by Dutton Children's Books,
a division of Penguin Putnam Books for Young Readers
345 Hudson Street, New York, New York 10014
www.penguinputnam.com
Designed by Sara Reynolds and Tim Hall
Music engraved by Bob Sherwin
Printed in Hong Kong
First Edition
1 3 5 7 9 10 8 6 4 2
ISBN: 0-525-45937-5

All of the songs contained in this book have been recorded
by José-Luis Orozco and are available on CD and cassette tape
from Arcoiris Records, Inc., P.O. Box 7428, Berkeley, CA 94707.
www.joseluisorozco.com

PREFACE

Latin American cultures contain a treasure trove of songs that celebrate the holidays and festivals that occur throughout the year. In an effort to preserve this varied and vivid tradition of words and music and transmit it to a new generation, I have compiled this volume of rhymes and songs, all of which I have shared with students and their parents as well as with teachers. In selecting them, I have tried to include samples that are representative of the diversity of Latin American culture and to choose songs with catchy rhythms and lyrics that are at once easy to teach and easy and fun to learn. Many of the selections are traditional, both in melody and language. With some I have taken the liberty of adapting the lyrics to fit a particular celebration.

Latino culture is very family-oriented and welcomes any occasion to get people together. I hope this collection will provide a good excuse to gather with your family, friends, and neighbors to celebrate throughout the year.

Now it's time for the fiestas!

J.-L. O.

Las palomitas ✳ The Doves

A traditional Argentine rhyme

Las palomitas del campo
nacieron para volar.
Mi corazón nació libre
y alegre para cantar.

The doves in the country
were born to fly.
My heart was born free
and happy to sing.

CONTENTS

✳

Los meses del año ✳ The Months of the Year

El Año Nuevo (*The New Year*) celebration, the first holiday of the year, starts exactly at midnight, with twelve rings of church bells marking the twelve months of the new year. Some people welcome the new year by eating one grape for each of the twelve bell rings. Friends and relatives embrace with best wishes for a Feliz Año Nuevo, or Happy New Year. Others take to the streets to sing and dance and bang pots and pans. In some countries, people set off small fireworks made from figurines filled with dry hay, representing the old year. This song is an adaptation of a traditional Caribbean tune with a merengue rhythm to which everybody can sing and dance.

Pa - lo, pa - lo, pa - lo, pa - lo, bo - ni - to, pa - lo,

é, aé, aé, aé, pa-lo, bo - ni- to, pa-lo, é. Pa-lo, pa-lo,

é. E - ne - ro, fe - bre - ro, mar-zo, a-bril y ma-yo, son los cin-co

me - ses pri - me - ros del a - ño. E - ne - ro, fe - a - ño.

Palo, palo, palo,
palo, bonito, palo, é,
aé, aé, aé
palo, bonito, palo, é.
[*cantar dos veces*]

Enero, febrero,
marzo, abril y mayo,
son los cinco meses,
primeros del año.
[*cantar dos veces*]

CORO
Palo, palo, palo . . .

Junio, julio, agosto,
septiembre, octubre,
noviembre y el último
mes es diciembre.

CORO
Palo, palo, palo . . .

Palo, palo, palo,
palo, bonito, palo, é
aé, aé, aé,
palo, bonito, palo, é.
[*sing twice*]

January, February,
March, April and May.
Let's enjoy this year
every single day.
[*sing twice*]

CHORUS
Palo, palo, palo . . .

June, July and August,
September, October,
November, December,
and this year is over.

CHORUS
Palo, palo, palo . . .

Los tres Reyes Magos ✳ The Three Wise Men

This is a song about three kings who, laden with gifts, followed a star in the eastern sky to find a special child of whose birth they had learned. The holiday, known as the Epiphany, is celebrated throughout the Spanish-speaking world on January 6. All children receive presents. As part of my family tradition, when I was a little boy, I wrote a letter to the three kings on January 5 asking for gifts. I put the letter in a shoe by the front door of our apartment. When I woke up on January 6, I was always surprised to find my shoe overflowing with toys or books. In the evening my family and friends got together for a small snack of hot chocolate, tamales, and rosca de reyes, a big cake shaped like a crown with a hole in the middle, decorated with jewel-like candied fruits.

Los tres Re - yes Ma - gos vie - nen del O - rien - te _____

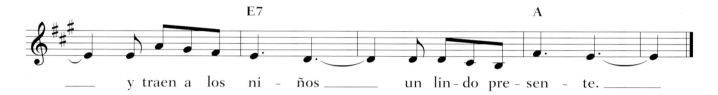

_____ y traen a los ni - ños _____ un lin - do pre - sen - te. _____

Los tres Reyes Magos vienen del Oriente y traen a los niños un lindo presente.	*The three kings are coming,* *they come from the Far East.* *They bring all the children* *baskets of gifts.*
Los tres Reyes Magos vienen de La Habana y traen a los niños sabrosa banana.	*The three kings are coming,* *they come from Havana.* *They bring all the children* *a tasty banana.*
Los tres Reyes Magos vienen de San Juan y traen a los niños lechita con pan.	*The three kings are coming,* *they come from San Juan.* *They bring all the children* *rice pudding and flan.*
Los tres Reyes Magos vienen de Caracas y traen a los niños congas y maracas.	*The three kings are coming* *they come from Caracas* *They bring all the children* *congas and maracas.*
Los tres Reyes Magos vienen desde Quito y traen a los niños un lindo librito.	*The three kings are coming,* *dancing the guaracha.* *They teach all the children* *the mambo and the cha-cha.*

El invierno ✳ Wintertime

January is the time when we all dress up for the cold in our ponchos, gloves, and boots and sing a lilting wintertime song to help keep ourselves warm. The melody comes from a Central American song called "Las estaciones," or "The Seasons." It is interesting to note that while it is wintertime in North America, it is summertime in some of the countries in South America, such as Chile, Argentina, and Uruguay.

Ya vie-ne el in-vier-no con frí-o y con hie-lo. Muy pron-to ca-e-rá mu-cha nie-ve del cie-lo. Ya cie-lo. Can-tar, can-tar que me con-ge-lo yo. Can-yo. Ya

Ya viene el invierno
con frío y con hielo.
Muy pronto caerá
mucha nieve del cielo

Cantar, cantar
que me congelo yo
[cantar dos veces]

*Wintertime is here,
with lots and lots of snow.
And the red nose of my burro,
again it's going to glow.*

*Let's sing, let's sing,
and play with the snow.*
[sing twice]

Mamá yo quiero ✳ Mama Paquita

Carnaval (Carnival) is a colorful celebration that takes place throughout Latin America right before Lent and the coming of spring. People celebrate in the streets for days with fancy costumes, parades, food, music, and dances. This Brazilian song of Carnaval is very well known in Latin America. You can form a conga line with your friends and relatives and start singing and dancing, just as they do during Carnaval!

Ma - má yo quie - ro Ma - má yo quie - ro, Ma -

má yo qui - e - ro ma - má a. Quie-ro la sam-ba, quie-ro la

rum-ba, quie-ro la sam - ba y la rum-ba pa'-bai - lar. Ma-má, ma-má, ma-má, yo

Mamá yo quiero	*Mama Paquita,*
Mamá yo quiero,	*Mama Paquita,*
Mamá yo quiero mamá.	*Mama, I like Carnival.*
Quiero la samba,	*I like the samba,*
quiero la rumba,	*I like the rumba,*
quiero la samba	*I like the samba*
y la rumba pa' bailar.	*and the rumba in Carnival.*
Mamá, mamá, mamá,	*Mama, Mama, Mama*
yo quiero	*Paquita.*
CORO	CHORUS
Mamá yo quiero, mamá . . .	*Mama, I like Carnival . . .*

El palomo y la paloma ✳ The Love Doves

On February 14, many people in the Americas celebrate Valentine's Day, or Día de los enamorados. The holiday, which is of European origin, includes an old tradition of sending a greeting card anonymously as a declaration of affection. This practice began in the sixteenth century on the feast day of a Roman priest and martyr, Saint Valentine, who was known as the patron saint of lovers. The following song celebrates love and friendship and is sung during the traditional Mexican Hat Dance, or jarabe tapatío, which comes from the state of Jalisco, Mexico.

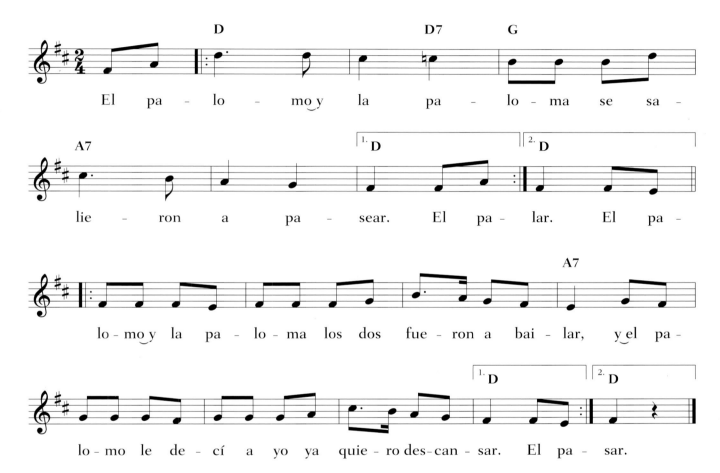

El pa - lo - mo y la pa - lo - ma se sa - lie - ron a pa - sear. El pa - lar. El pa - lo - mo y la pa - lo - ma los dos fue - ron a bai - lar, y el pa - lo - mo le de - cí - a yo ya quie - ro des-can - sar. El pa - sar.

El palomo y la paloma	Mister Dove and his sweetheart
se salieron a pasear	sauntered out to take a stroll.
el palomo le decía	She looked up and asked him sweetly,
vente que voy a bailar.	"Will you take me to the ball?"
El palomo y la paloma	Mister Dove and his sweetheart
los dos fueron a bailar,	both danced the whole night through.
y el palomo le decía	Mister Dove whispered, exhausted,
yo ya quiero descansar.	"That's enough for our debut."

La bella hortelana ✳ The Hardworking Farmer

"La bella hortelana" reminds us of the work that women have done for centuries to keep their families healthy and happy, many of them working in the fields or in their little plots and gardens, growing vegetables and fruits for the whole family. Corn is an important crop in Latin America, and this song celebrates its cycle. I dedicate this song to the celebration of International Women's Day on March 8. Vivan las mujeres! Long live all women!

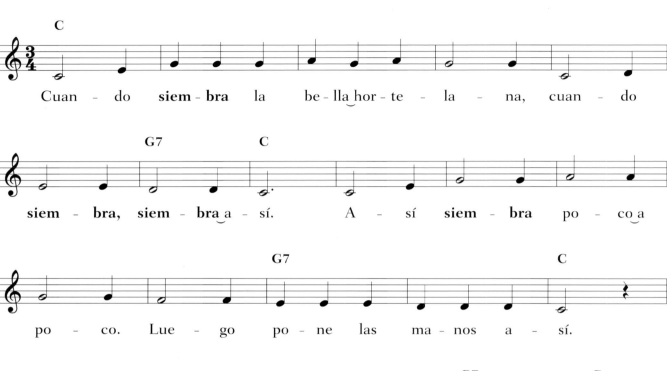

Cuan - do **siem - bra** la be - lla hor - te - la - na, cuan - do

siem - bra, siem - bra a - sí. A - sí **siem - bra** po - co a

po - co. Lue - go po - ne las ma - nos a - sí.

Siem - bra a - sí. Lue - go po - ne las ma - nos a - sí.

Cuando **siembra** la bella hortelana,
cuando **siembra**, **siembra** así.
Así **siembra** poco a poco.
Luego pone las manos así.
Siembra así.
Luego pone las manos así.

When the farmer takes care of her garden,
*when she **plants** corn, she **plants** it like this.*
*As she **plants** it little by little,*
she sings and claps like this.
*She **plants** it like this,*
then she sings and claps like this.

Repeat, replacing the words in boldface with one of the following phrases:

riega su maíz . . .
corta su maíz . . .
muele su maíz . . .
tortea (hace) sus tortillas . . .
coce sus tortillas . . .
sus tortillas . . .
come sus . . .

waters her corn . . .
harvests her corn . . .
grinds her corn . . .
makes her tortillas . . .
cooks her tortillas . . .
shares her tortillas . . .
eats her tortillas . . .

¡Viva César Chávez! ✳ Long Live Cesar Chavez!

Cesar Chavez was born on March 31, 1927, near Yuma, Arizona, to a farming family, and died on April 23, 1993. Chavez is best known for organizing the United Farm Workers union in the state of California. He led marches and went on hunger strikes to emphasize the need to improve the living and working conditions of the farmworkers. His struggle had a great impact all over the United States, as the union was able to accomplish many of its goals to bring justice and dignity to the men, women, and children who labor in the fields.

Many schools, parks, libraries, and streets throughout the United States bear this courageous man's name, and the state of California has declared March 31 Cesar Chavez Day. We, too, can join our voices together and honor him with this call-and-response chant.

¡Viva César Chávez!	*Long live Cesar Chavez!*
¡Viva César Chávez!	*Long live Cesar Chavez!*
Lider campesino.	*Leader of the farmworkers.*
Luchaste por los niños,	*You fought for the children,*
Luchaste por los pobres,	*You fought for the poor,*
Luchaste por los sueldos,	*You fought for better wages,*
Luchaste por dignidad,	*You fought for dignity,*
Ayunaste muchas veces,	*You fasted many times,*
Marchaste con la gente,	*You marched with the people,*
Dijiste ¡Sí se puede!	*You said, "Yes we can!"*
Dijiste **¡Sí se puede!**	*You said **¡Sí se puede!***

For call-and-response, a person or group sings a line, then a second person or group repeats the same line. Repeat the words in boldface seven times, each time saying the words a little faster and clapping your hands for each syllable.

Este niño lindo ✳ My Sweet Baby

In the twentieth century, countries of the world concerned about the rights, welfare, education, and health of all children began to create programs for them with established international organizations and started celebrating the International Day of the Child. Many Latin American countries celebrate the day on April 30 to coincide with the celebration of the "Week of the Book." "Este niño lindo" is a lullaby or cradle song that shows our love and affection for every child all over the world.

Es - te ni - ño lin - do se quie - re dor - mir.

Há - gan - le su cu - na en un to - ron - jíl.

Este niño lindo
se quiere dormir.
Háganle su cuna
en un toronjíl.

Esta niña linda
que nació de noche.
Quiere que la lleven
a pasear en coche.

*Rest my little baby,
I'll rock you to sleep.
I will make your cradle
on this little leaf.*

*Oh, my pretty baby,
you were born at night.
Let your mama rock you
in her car tonight.*

Cinco de mayo ✳ Cinco de Mayo

Cinco de Mayo, or May 5, is an important holiday in schools and communities of Latin America and the United States, where its celebration is growing more and more widespread. On this date in 1862, the Mexican army, under the command of General Ignacio Zaragoza and with the help of the Mexican people, defeated French troops near the city of Puebla, proving that they could protect their country from foreign invaders. Benito Juárez, president of Mexico at that time, said, "Entre los individuos como entre las naciones, el respeto al derecho ajeno es la paz." ("Respect for the rights of others must go hand in hand with peace.") The music for this song is taken from the traditional Mexican song "La cucaracha."

Cin-co de ma-yo, cin-co de ma-yo, ce-le-bre-mos co-mo her-

ma-nos la gran vic-to-ria que es un or-gu-llo, pa-ra el pue-blo me-xi-ca-no.

¡Vi-va Don Be-ni-to Juá-rez! ¡Vi-va Ig-na-cio Za-ra-go-za!

¡Vi-va el pue-blo de va-lien-tes! A-llá en Pue-bla, la glo-rio-sa!

Cinco de mayo, cinco de mayo,
celebremos como hermanos
la gran victoria que es un orgullo
para el pueblo mexicano.
[canta dos veces]

¡Viva Don Benito Juárez!
¡Viva Ignacio Zaragoza!
¡Viva el pueblo de valientes!
Allá en Puebla, la gloriosa.

Cinco de Mayo, Cinco de Mayo,
let us celebrate the day.
A day of victory, a day of pride
for the country, Mexico.
[sing twice]

Long live Don Benito Juárez!
Viva Ignacio Zaragoza!
Brave and dedicated people
who defended us in Puebla.

CORO
Cinco de mayo, cinco de mayo . . .

Es la hora de la fiesta,
alegría y canciones,
¡Viva el cinco de mayo
que alegra los corazones!

Cinco de mayo, cinco de mayo,
celebremos como hermanos
la gran victoria que es un orgullo
para el pueblo mexicano.

Vivan todos los valientes
que nos dieron libertad
para que en el mundo haya
más justicia y dignidad.

CORO
Cinco de mayo, cinco de mayo . . .

Año de mil ochocientos sesenta y dos,
sí señores, en la batalla de Puebla
cayeron los invasores.

CORO
Cinco de mayo, cinco de mayo . . .

[hablado]

¡Viva México! ¡Viva el cinco de mayo!
Con esta gran celebración
recordamos las célebres palabras
del Presidente Benito Juárez:

"Entre los individuos,
como entre las naciones,
el respeto al derecho ajeno es la paz."

CHORUS
Cinco de Mayo, Cinco de Mayo . . .

It is the time for celebration,
time for singing, time for dancing.
Viva el Cinco de Mayo,
let us join in the fiesta!

Cinco de Mayo, Cinco de Mayo,
we celebrate our brotherhood,
our proud victory—
victory for our people.

Long live all those valiant heroes
who defended us in Puebla.
Freedom, dignity, and justice
make the world a better place.

CHORUS
Cinco de Mayo, Cinco de Mayo . . .

In the year of 1862,
yes, at the Battle of Puebla,
the invaders were defeated.

CHORUS
Cinco de Mayo, Cinco de Mayo . . .

[spoken]

Long live Mexico! Long live Cinco de Mayo!
With this great celebration
remember the wise words
of President Benito Juárez:

"Respect among people,
respect among nations,
brings peace."

La maestra ✳ My Teacher

I wrote this song to honor all my teachers. The day on which National Teacher Day is celebrated varies from country to country. In Mexico, it is celebrated on May 15 and in the United States on the Tuesday of the first full week of May. This particular song starts and ends with a porra, or cheer.

A la bio,   a la bao,   a la bim, bom, ba,   la ma-

es-tra,   la ma-es-tra,   ra, ra, ra. Con ca - ri-ño y a - le-grí - a   ce-le-

bra-mos es - te dí - a   de-di - ca-do a la ma - es - tra que tra-

ba - ja no-che y dí - a.   Nos en - se - ña a le - er,   a su-

mar y a res - tar,   a ser bue-nos es - tu - dian-tes y tam-

bién a res-pe-tar.   A la bi - o bi - o bi - o, a la

bi - o   bi - o   ba,   la ma - es - tra,   la ma - es - tra,   la ma -

es - tra,   ra,   ra,   ra.   A   la   es - tra,   ra,   ra,   ra. _____

[porra]

A la bio, a la bao,
a la bim, bom, ba.
La maestra, la maestra,
ra, ra, ra.

[cancíon]

Con cariño y alegría
celebramos este día
dedicado a la maestra
que trabaja noche y día.

Nos enseña a leer,
a sumar y a restar,
a ser buenos estudiantes
y también a respetar.

[porra]

A la bio . . .

[cheer]

A la bio, a la bao,
a la bim, bom, ba.
My teacher, my teacher,
rah, rah, rah.

[song]

With love and happiness
we celebrate this great day,
honoring our teacher
who works with us night and day.

She teaches us to read,
how to add and to subtract,
how to be good students,
to respect and how to act.

[cheer]

A la bio . . .

¡Que bonita bandera! ✳ My Puerto Rican Flag!

The Puerto Rican flag has five stripes, three red and two white, and a white star that represents Puerto Rico inside a blue triangle. It was designed at the end of the nineteenth century by a group of Puerto Rican patriots who wanted their native land to be independent from Spain. This song is a version of a very popular song that is sung year-round during fiestas and parades, both in Puerto Rico and the United States. One of these celebrations, La Fiesta de San Juan (Saint John the Baptist), occurs on June 24. We can join with Puerto Rican schoolchildren in celebrating their flag, as well as the flags of all the countries of the Americas and of the world.

Que bo-ni - ta ban - de - ra, que bo-ni - ta ban - de - ra,

que bo-ni - ta ban - de-ra es la ban - de-ra **puer - to-ri - que-ña.**

Que bonita bandera,
que bonita bandera
que bonita bandera,
es la bandera **puertorriqueña**.

*Let's all sing to the pretty flag,
let's all sing to the pretty flag,
let's all sing to the pretty flag,
the pretty flag from* **Puerto Rico**.

Repeat the song, replacing the word in boldface with one of the following words (or choose a different country).

mexicana   *Mexico*
salvadoreña   *El Salvador*
colombiana   *Colombia*
guatemalteca   *Guatemala*
argentina   *Argentina*
cubana, etc.   *Cuba, etc.*

¡Viva mi barrio! ✳ Long Live My Neighborhood!

I wrote this song for all the children from the barrios to inspire self-esteem and high expectations and to urge kids not to forget the neighborhoods they came from when they grow up. This is a very appropriate song for graduation time or for the beginning of the school year. ¡Viva mi barrio!

So-mos los ni-ños del ba - rrio, los ni-ños tra-ba - ja-do-res. res. Va - mos a ser pro - fe - so-res ___ y tam - bién go - ber - na - do - res. ___ Va - mos res. Que vi - va vi - va mi ba - rrio ___ con Jua - na, Je - sús y Ma - rio. ___ Que - rio.

Somos los niños del barrio,	*We are the kids from the barrio,*
los niños trabajadores.	*children of hardworking people.*
[cantar dos veces]	*[sing twice]*
Vamos a ser profesores	*Some of us will be great teachers,*
y también gobernadores.	*some of us will be great leaders.*
[cantar dos veces]	*[sing twice]*

CORO
¡Que viva, viva mi barrio . . .
con Juana, Jesús y Mario.
[cantar dos veces]

Todas las niñas del barrio,
son niñas trabajadoras,
[cantar dos veces]

unas seran abogadas
y otras van a ser doctoras.
[cantar dos veces]

CORO
¡Que viva, viva mi barrio . . .

Y ya cuando seamos grandes
al barrio regresaremos,
[cantar dos veces]

todos los profesionistas
a la gente ayudaremos.
[cantar dos veces]

CORO
¡Que viva, viva mi barrio . . .

CHORUS
Long live, long live my barrio,
with Juana, Jesse, and Mario!
[sing twice]

We are the kids from the barrio,
children of hardworking people.
[sing twice]

We will soon become good lawyers,
good pilots, dentists, and doctors.
[sing twice]

CHORUS
Long live, long live my barrio . . .

When we all finish college,
we'll share our good, strong hands
[sing twice]

with the people in the barrios,
in the barrios of this land.
[sing twice]

CHORUS
Long live, long live my barrio . . .

Arroz con leche ✳ Rice Pudding

Traditionally, after a church wedding ceremony, guests and relatives shower the bride and groom with rice. Rice pudding is often served at wedding receptions. In one of the most popular children's games in Latin America, children make a circle, alternating boys and girls. The boys clap and sing the first part of the song. Then the girls face the boys and sing the second part of the song, clapping as they sing.

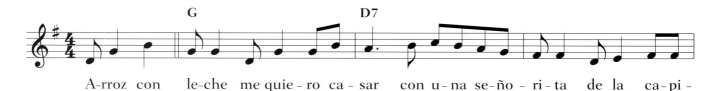

A-rroz con le-che me quie-ro ca-sar con u-na se-ño-ri-ta de la ca-pi-

tal que se-pa co-ser, que se-pa bor-dar, que se-pa a-brir la

puer-ta pa-ra ir a ju-gar. Con-ti-go sí, con-ti-go

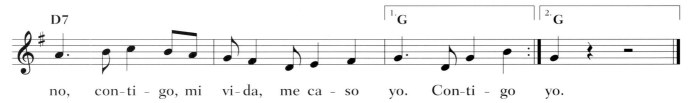

no, con-ti-go, mi vi-da, me ca-so yo. Con-ti-go yo.

Arroz con leche
me quiero casar
con una señorita
de la capital
que sepa coser,
que sepa bordar,
que sepa abrir la puerta
para ir a jugar.

Contigo sí,
contigo no,
contigo, mi vida,
me caso yo.

Rice pudding, rice pudding,
I want to get married
to a señorita
who lives on the hill.
She'll know how to sew,
she'll know how to cook,
and she will enjoy
a walk in the park.

Are you the right one?
Maybe you're not.
With you, my sweetheart,
I will tie the knot.

La quinceañera ✳ The Quinceañera

On a girl's fifteenth birthday, she celebrates her quinceañera. At this fiesta she is pre-
sented to the community as an adult with a special religious ceremony as well as a special dance party. This song is an adaptation of a traditional song in which each person
takes a turn dancing inside a circle of dancers.

La quin-ce a - ñe - ra es - ta - ba en el bai - le que lo

bai - le que lo bai - le tan lin - da y tan be - lla pa - re - ce u - na

rei - na. Que pa - se us - ted que la quie-ro ver bai - lar al -

zan-do los pies en el ai - re pe-ro bien que lo bai-la us - ted. Dé-jen-la

so - la, so-la en el bai - le la, la, la, la, la, la, la, la, la,

la, la, la, ra, la, la, la, la, la, ra, la, la, la, la.

La quinceañera estaba en el baile
que lo baile que lo baile.
Tan linda y tan bella
parece una reina.

Que pase usted
que la quiero ver bailar.
Alzando los pies en el aire
pero bien que lo baila usted.
Déjenla sola, sola en el baile.

La, la, la, la, la, la,
la, la, la, la, la, la.
La, ra, la, la, la, la, la, la,
la, ra, la, la, la, la.
[cantar dos veces]

Here comes the quinceañera,
she's coming into the ballroom.
Swing and start the dancing.
So beautiful and graceful,
she looks just like a queen.

Now take your place.
We want to see you dance.
Tap your heels and toes,
swing and swing and swing.
Oh, what a treat to see you dancing.

La, la, la, la, la, la,
la, la, la, la, la, la.
La, ra, la, la, la, la,
la, ra, la, la, la, la.
[sing twice]

Corre, niño ✳ Run, Run, Children

My parents often sang this song when my brothers and sisters and I were getting ready to go to school early in the morning. It is a very well-known song in Latin America.

Corre, co-rre, ni-ño, pa-ja-ri-tos vue-lan, que las es-tre-

lli-tas ya es-tán en la es-cue-la. La ma-es-tra lu-na dic-ta la lec-

ción y u-na nu-be ne-gra es el pi-za-rrón. ja.

Corre, corre, niño,
pajaritos vuelan,
que las estrellitas
ya están en la escuela.

La maestra luna
dicta la lección
y una nube negra
es el pizarrón.

Un trozo de cielo
es el borrador
borra el que siempre
se porta mejor.

Una estrellita
se llenó de tiza
y todas las otras
se mueren de risa,
ja, ja, ja, ja, ja, ja
ja, ja, ja, ja, ja,
ja, ja, ja, ja, ja, ja
ja, ja, ja, ja, ja.

Run, run, children,
little birds are flying.
All the little stars
have now gone to school.

The moon is their teacher,
giving the first lesson.
The cloud in the classroom,
we call it the chalkboard.

From the sky a piece fell.
It was the eraser.
All the children used it
to get rid of errors.

A tiny little star
got covered with chalk dust.
All the other students
thought it was a joke, ha!
Ha, ha, ha, ha, ha, ha,
ha, ha, ha, ha, ha.
Ha, ha, ha, ha, ha, ha,
ha, ha, ha, ha, ha.

Día de la Raza ✳ Brotherhood Day

On October 12 we remember Christopher Columbus's encounter with the Native Americans on the islands of the Caribbean. This day marks the beginning of a new "race" in the Americas as many cultures began to mix. It is celebrated in the Americas with Native American chants, dances, parades, and fiestas.

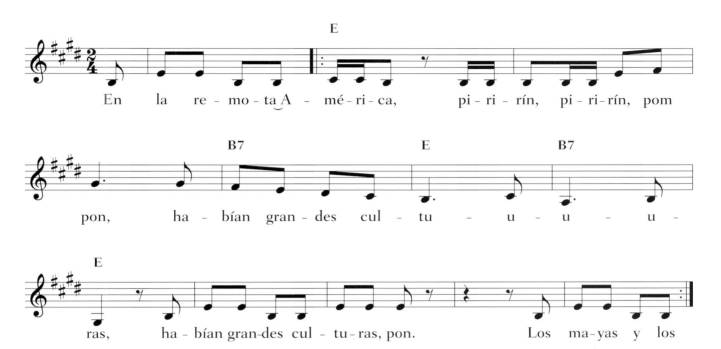

En la remota América,
piririn, piririn, pom pon,
habían grandes culturas
habían grandes culturas, pon.

Los mayas y los incas,
piririn, piririn, pom pon,
y muchos, muchos más,
y muchos, muchos más, pon.

Sabían mucho de ciencia,
piririn, piririn, pom pon,
y eran grandes artistas,
y eran grandes artistas, pon.

In the old Americas,
piririn, piririn, pom pon,
great cultures lived,
great cultures lived, pon.

The Mayans and the Incas,
piririn, piririn, pom pon,
and many, many more,
and many, many more, pon.

They were great scientists,
piririn, piririn, pom pon,
and they were artists too,
and they were artists too, pon.

Un día en Atlántico,
piririn, piririn, pom pon,
tres barcos se perdieron,
tres barcos se perdieron, pon.

De España habían salido,
piririn, piririn, pom pon,
con Cristobal Colón,
con Cristobal Colón, pon.

Por cosas del destino,
piririn, piririn, pom pon,
llegaron al Caribe,
llegaron al Caribe, pon.

El doce de octubre,
piririn, piririn, pom pon,
de mil cuatrocientos noventa y dos,
de mil cuatrocientos noventa y dos, pon.

Con los que aquí estaban,
piririn, piririn, pom pon,
y los que iban llegando,
y los que iban llegando, pon.

Se hizo un arcoiris,
piririn, piririn, pom pon,
de personas muy lindas,
de personas muy lindas, pon.

El cuento aquí se acaba,
piririn, piririn, pom pon,
del Día de la Raza,
del Día de la Raza, pon.

Como ya está acabado,
piririn, piririn, pom pon,
volvemos a empezar,
volvemos a empezar, pon.

One day in the Atlantic,
piririn, piririn, pom pon,
three little boats were lost,
three little boats were lost, pon.

They came from far away,
piririn, piririn, pom pon
with Christopher Columbus,
with Christopher Columbus, pon.

Their destiny was charted,
piririn, piririn, pom pon,
to the Caribbean they arrived,
to the Caribbean they arrived, pon.

On the twelfth of October,
piririn, piririn, pom pon,
fourteen hundred ninety-two,
fourteen hundred ninety-two, pon.

With the people from the Americas,
piririn, piririn, pom pon,
and those who were arriving,
and those who were arriving, pon.

A great rainbow was forming,
piririn, piririn, pom pon,
of good-looking people,
of good-looking people, pon.

The story has just ended,
piririn, piririn, pom pon,
of the day of brotherhood,
the day of brotherhood, pon.

Since it's already finished,
piririn, piririn, pom pon,
I'll tell you once again,
I'll tell you once again, pon.

Tumbas ✳ Tombs

On *Noche de brujas (Night of the Witches)*, *or Halloween, instead of carving pumpkins, my friends and I attached a string to a cardboard box, decorated it with a scary face, and put a candle inside. Then, donning our simple costumes, we toured our neighborhood house by house, asking for* una calavera—*candy, fruit, or money. "Tumbas" is a chant for* Noche de brujas. *It is sung with a deep voice and a jump with each "heh" at the end of the song.*

En – tre las rui – nas de un mon – as – te – rio se a – bren las

puer – tas de un ce-men – te – rio. Tum-bas por a – quí, tum-bas por a –

llá, tum – bas y tum – bas, ja, ja, ja, ja, ja. Tum-bas por a –

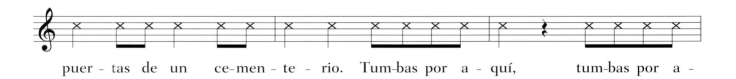

quí, tum-bas por a – llá, tum-bas y tum-bas, ja, ja, ja, ja, ja.

Entre las ruinas de un monasterio
se abren las puertas de un cemetario.
Tumbas por aquí, tumbas por allá,
tumbas y tumbas,
ja, ja, ja, ja, ja.

*Deep in the ruins of a dark monastery,
the doors open slowly in the old cemetery.
Tombs over there, tombs over there,
tombs and more tombs,
heh, heh, heh, heh, heh.*

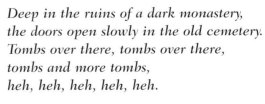

NOVIEMBRE • NOVEMBER

Día de los muertos ✳ Day of the Dead

The Day of the Dead, or Día de los muertos, is a very old tradition in Latin American countries. Every year, on November 1 and 2, people gather, at home and in the cemetery, to remember departed loved ones and to celebrate their lives with music, prayer, food, and a special offering called ofrendas or altares, which includes incense, sugar skulls, pan de muerto (special bread made for the occasion), pictures, food, and drink.

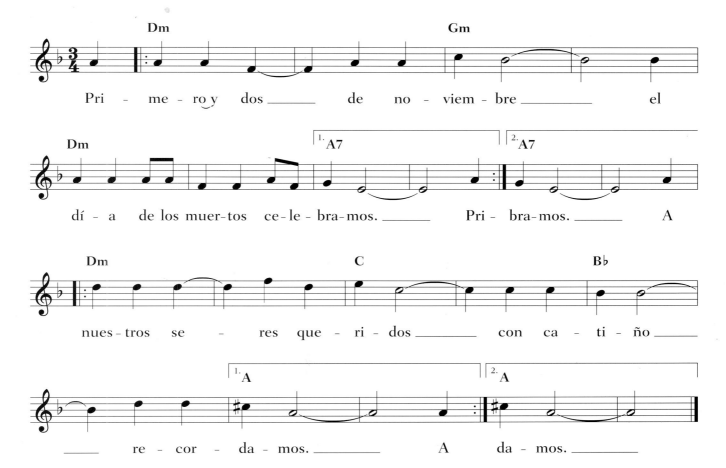

Primero y dos de noviembre
el día de los muertos celebramos
a nuestros seres queridos
con cariño recordamos.

Cuando llegue el día de los muertos
haremos un altar bonito
con copal y muchas flores
para todos los muertitos.

Llevaremos pan de muerto
con tamales y atolito,
calabacitas con chile,
también mole con pollito.

*On November first and second,
we honor those who've departed.
With music and with prayer,
we celebrate Day of the Dead.*

*On that special day,
we collect offerings for our altar
of incense and many flowers
for all our beloved departed.*

*We'll bring them pan de muertos,
some tamales and atolito,
green squash with chili pepper,
chicken mole and taquitos.*

Pozole para los muertos,
tortillas y frijolitos,
calaveritas de azúcar,
fruta fresca y juguetitos.

Con las velas encendidas
el día de los muertos celebramos.
A nuestros seres queridos
les cantamos y rezamas.

Pozole for our dear ones,
tortillas and pinto beans,
sweet sugar confections,
fresh fruit and little toys.

With all the candles glowing,
we celebrate their memory always.
With food and song and prayer,
we celebrate Day of the Dead.

Damos gracias ✳ Thanksgiving

Día de dar gracias, or Thanksgiving, is a special celebration of the fall harvest when we give thanks to Mother Earth. At home we celebrate with Native American foods like squash (calabaza), turkey (guajolote), products made from corn (maíz) like tamales, tostadas, and atole (a delicious drink made with cornmeal).

A la madre tierra damos gracias
por el alimento que nos da.
Damos gracias, damos gracias
por nuestra salud y bienestar.

*To our Mother Earth we are thankful
for the food we get from her bounty.
We are thankful, we are thankful
for our prosperity and good health.*

Mañanitas Guadalupanas ✳ Morning Song to Our Lady of Guadalupe

On December 12, 1531, on the hill of Tepeyac, just north of downtown Mexico City (close to where I grew up), a brown-skinned Virgin Mary appeared before Juan Diego, a poor peasant. After Juan Diego prayed to this vision, his ailing uncle was miraculously healed. According to many people, she performed other miracles. A big temple was built in her honor, and every year on this day, Aztec dancers perform the old rituals, mariachis sing "Las Mañanitas," and millions of people from all over come to worship the Virgin. She is known as the Virgin of Guadalupe, after a similar dark-skinned vision that appeared in the town of Guadalupe, Spain.

O, Vir - gen la más her - mo - sa del va - lle del A -

ná - huac, tus hi - jos muy de ma - ña - na te vie - nen

a sa - lu - dar. Des - pier - ta, Ma - dre, des -

pier - ta, mi - ra que ya a - ma - ne - cío, ya los

pa - ja - ri - llos can - tan, la lu - na ya se me - tío.

O, Virgen la más hermosa
del valle del Anáhuac,
tus hijos muy de mañana
te vienen a saludar.

Despierta, Madre, despierta,
mira que ya amaneció,
ya los pajarillos cantan,
la luna ya se metió.

O, brillante lucerito
que alumbrando al Tepeyác
diste luz a Juan Dieguito
en su humilde caminar.

CORO
Despierta, Madre, despierta . . .

Ya la aurora se levanta
canta alegre el ruiseñor
y tu pueblo con cariño
a coro ensalza tu honor.

CORO
Despierta, Madre, despierta . . .

Dear Virgin of Guadalupe,
from the valley of Anáhuac,
listen to our song and prayer
that now we sing to you.

Awaken, Mother, awaken
and look at the bright new day.
All the little birds are singing,
and the moon has gone away.

O, beautiful and bright star
who shines over Tepeyác,
you gave light to Juan Dieguito
in the Valley of Anáhuac.

CHORUS
Awaken, Mother, awaken . . .

The bright sun is coming out,
and the nightingale will sing.
Hear the voices of your people,
they are here to honor you.

CHORUS
Awaken, Mother, awaken . . .

Las posadas ✳ The Shelter

"Las posadas" is a song depicting the journey of Mary and Joseph as they sought shelter shortly before the birth of the baby Jesus. This journey is celebrated with a procession accompanied by songs, prayer, food, and the breaking of a piñata. The procession winds through the town, and the singers call out to the villagers, asking for shelter.

En el nom-bre ___ del cie - lo os ___ pi - do ___ po -

sa - da pues ___ no pue-de an-dar ___

mi ___ es - po - sa a - ma - - - da. ___

En - tren san - tos pe - re - gri - nos, pe - re -

gri - nos, re - ci - ban es - te rin - cón. Aun-que es zón.

Hu - mil-des pe - re - gri - nos Je - sús, Ma-ría y Jo - sé, mi

al - ma doy con e - llos, mi co - ra-zón tam-bién. Hu - bién.

En el nombre del cielo
os pido posada
pues no puede andar
mi esposa amada.

Aquí no es mesón,
sigan adelante.
Pues no puedo abrir
no sea algún tunante.

No seas inhumano
danos caridad
que el Dios de los Cielos
se los premiará.

¿Quién viene a esta hora,
el sueño a turbar?
Váyanse de aquí
para otro lugar.

Venimos rendidos
desde Nazaréth.
Yo soy carpintero
de nombre José.

No me importa el nombre
déjenme dormir.
Pues yo les digo
que no hemos de abrir.

Posada te pide
amado casero
por solo una noche
la Reina del Cielo.

Pues si es una reina
quien lo solicita,
¿Cómo es que de noche
anda tan solita?

Mi esposa es María,
la Reina del Cielo
y madre va a ser
del Divino Verbo.

Eres tú José,
tu esposa es María.
Entren peregrinos
no los conocía.

In the name of Heaven
I ask you for shelter,
since my lovely wife
is about to give birth.

This is not an inn,
go away.
I can't open the door,
how do I know you are not a thief?

Please don't be cruel,
show us some human kindness.
And our God in Heaven
will reward you well.

Who comes knocking at this hour,
who is disturbing my sleep?
Go away from here
to some other place.

Our walk has been too long,
we've walked from Nazareth.
I am a carpenter,
and my name is Joseph.

I don't care who you are,
just let me sleep.
I am telling you
that we won't open the door.

The Queen of Heaven
is asking only for shelter.
Just let us stay one night
under your roof tonight.

If it's a queen
who is making the request,
how is it that on this night
she is all alone?

My wife is Mary,
the Queen of Heaven
and the mother-to-be
of the King of Earth.

You are Joseph,
and your wife is Mary.
Please come in, dear pilgrims.
I did not recognize you.

Dios pague señores
vuestra caridad
y los colme el cielo
de felicidad.

Entren santos peregrinos,
peregrinos,
reciban este rincón.
Aunque es pobre la morada,
la morada,
es grande mi corazón.

Humildes peregrinos
Jesús, María y José,
mi alma doy con ellos,
mi corazón también.

[cantar dos veces]

May God repay all your kindness,
and may Heaven bless you
with celestial happiness
for now and forever.

Come in, you holy pilgrims,
holy pilgrims.
You are welcome to rest here.
Although our house is humble,
our house is humble,
we warmly welcome you.

These humble pilgrims
Jesus, Mary, and Joseph,
my soul I give to them.
I give my heart as well.

[sing twice]

SUBJECT INDEX

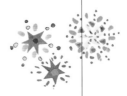